E   Rand, Gloria
R   Salty sails north.   Illus. by Ted
C.1   Rand.   Holt, 1990.
                n.p.   col. illus.

I. Title.

SALTY
SAILS NORTH

GLORIA RAND
Illustrated by TED RAND

Henry Holt and Company • New York

In loving memory of Gloria's father, Roy E. Kistler,
a true lover of books.
Special thanks to Chris and Dick Marshall for sharing
their experiences sailing north to Alaska in the 26-foot
sailboat *Sequin*. Special thanks also to nautical advisors
Dr. Robert C. Coe and W. Hunter Simpson.

Text copyright © 1990 by Gloria Rand
Illustrations copyright © 1990 by Ted Rand
All rights reserved, including the right to reproduce
this book or portions thereof in any form.
Published by Henry Holt and Company, Inc.
115 West 18th Street, New York, New York 10011.
Published in Canada by Fitzhenry & Whiteside Limited,
195 Allstate Parkway, Markham, Ontario L3R 4T8.

Library of Congress Cataloging-in-Publication Data
Rand, Gloria.
   Salty sails North / Gloria Rand : illustrated by Ted Rand.
   Summary: Salty the dog and his master Zack sail north to
Alaska, encountering other ships, a storm, wild animals on the
shore, and an iceberg.
   ISBN 0-8050-1160-9
   [1. Sailing—Fiction.   2. Dogs—Fiction.]   I. Rand, Ted, ill.
II. Title.
PZ7.R1553San   1990
[E]—dc20   89-39063

Henry Holt books are available at special discounts
for bulk purchases for sales promotions, premiums,
fund-raising, or educational use. Special editions
or book excerpts can also be created to specification.

   For details contact:

   Special Sales Director
   Henry Holt and Company, Inc.
   115 West 18th Street
   New York, New York 10011

First Edition
Designed by Victoria Hartman
Printed in the United States of America
10 9 8 7 6 5 4 3 2 1

SALTY
SAILS NORTH

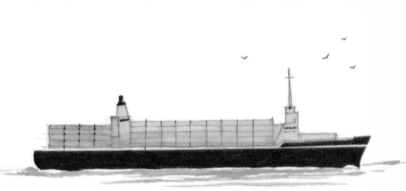

Look sharp!" Zack shouted to Salty one summer day. "We're on our way to Alaska."

Salty scampered up to the boat's bow, his favorite place to ride. He had been a puppy when Zack had built this boat. Now he was a grown-up deep-sea sailor, a real salty dog.

A huge container ship passed by, and Salty barked a sharp warning.

"Good crew," Zack called out. "We're going to see lots of boats as we head north. I need you to be my lookout."

And they did see lots of boats. They saw cruise ships, private yachts, car and passenger ferries. They saw freighters, fishing boats, and tugs towing barges. Whenever a ship came into view, Salty raced around the deck, barking. The bigger the boat, the louder he barked.

"Cool it, slow down," Zack scolded Salty one day.
"You're going to fall overboard if you aren't careful."

"Looks like a squall is headed our way," Zack warned Salty late one afternoon. "Let's put our life vests and lifelines on right now. Okay, Old Salt?"

Zack quickly helped Salty into his gear, then hurried to tie down the boom and close the hatch. Salty was jumping around, right on Zack's heels.

"Stop it, Salty!" Zack yelled. But Salty didn't obey. He ran to the edge of the boat. "No, Salty! Out of my way!" Zack pushed Salty into a corner of the boat's open cockpit. "Now, stay," he said.

Zack and Salty rode out the storm. As they made their way safely into a sheltered bay, Zack said, "Sorry I yelled at you, Salty, but at sea you must learn to obey my orders. That was a tough situation out there."

Salty shook the rain and seawater off his thick coat and wagged his tail.

The next morning the skies cleared and the sun was shining.

"Time for a little shore leave," Zack announced. They rowed to a small, forested island. "You've never been in deep woods."

While Zack tied the boat's dinghy to a tree, Salty ran up and down the forest trail, yelping as loudly as he could, just for fun.

From off in the distance came an answering
howl.

"That you?" Zack turned toward Salty
slowly, carefully looking in all directions.
Salty did not move.

A large gray wolf stood at the edge of a
nearby bluff. He did not move either, but
just stared down at Zack and Salty. He
stared and stared, then silently vanished
into the forest.

"We've got to get out of here. Who knows
how many wolves are up there," Zack
whispered.

Zack didn't have to tell Salty twice. Salty
trotted right along close against Zack's legs
as they quickly headed back down the trail.

Safely aboard their boat, Zack hugged his
dog. "How did you know to not chase
wolves?"

Sailing up the coast was never lonely for
Zack and Salty. Gulls followed their boat,
and eagles watched from high overhead.
Sea lions, seals, whales, and porpoises often
swam alongside. On stops, they found
abandoned fish canneries, deserted mines,
and even totem poles standing at the
water's edge and deep in the forests.

One day they discovered a Tlingit tribe's ancient longhouse.

Rowing ashore, Zack pointed to a totem pole. Many years before, it had identified the Indian clan who lived there.

"This cedar plank house was once a home and a fort," Zack told Salty. "Many families lived in one building. They held feasts, religious ceremonies, and dances inside. We'll tie up to a log right where the Indians used to pull in their canoes. And then let's go in."

Salty followed Zack as he stooped to enter the only doorway, a low entrance facing the water. The house was dark and empty, just patches of daylight coming in through broken planks. Inside, it had a damp, woodsy smell. The dug-out center no longer had cedar floors covered with cedar mats. The platforms along each side of the building, where people had once sat, slept, and kept their storage boxes, had crumbled. The chief's quarters, at the end of the large room, had fallen down. Near that wall was a hole covered with planks, a Tlingit Indian foot drum.

"Sure don't want to leave," Zack told Salty. "But I've charted a long sail. We have to go."

For the next few days the winds were strong, and the little sailboat made good time to an isolated cove. A fisherman waved from the shore.

"Cleaning the catch," he called. "Got some fresh fish for ya!"

Salty jumped out of the dinghy as soon as it reached the beach.

"Hey, hold on to that dog. There are bears around here—a mama and her cubs, I think," the fisherman warned.

Zack wasted no time calling Salty back. "Good boy," he praised Salty, taking a firm hold of his collar.

"The most dangerous animal in the world is a mama grizzly with hungry cubs," the fisherman explained. "Here's how you know they're around," he added, pointing to a patch of uprooted skunk cabbage. "That's any bear's favorite salad."

The fisherman left his fish scraps on the beach for the wild animals. "Nothing goes to waste in the wilderness," he told Zack and Salty.

As Zack rowed back to the sailboat, there was a low growl from Salty. He was trembling with excitement as he looked toward land.

On shore stood a big grizzly bear peering over low shoreline bushes. Cautiously she moved out onto the beach and pulled the fish scraps back from the tide line just as a pair of cubs raced out for dinner.

"Some adventure! Bears that close are *too* close, even for me," Zack laughed. "Glad you came back when I called you, Old Salt. Even a brave dog couldn't win a bear fight."

Salty kept watching the bears.

Late the next evening Zack and Salty
motored into a large bay filled with white
dots.

"Just ice," Zack called out to Salty, who was
yelping at all the passing ghosts. "Calm
down."

"The little chunks are harmless," Zack
explained. "Bigger pieces are icebergs."

Lowering the anchor, Zack worried out
loud. "One of those icebergs could crush
our boat if it hit just right. Better stay here
until morning. We have a wind that should
blow them away from us—I hope."

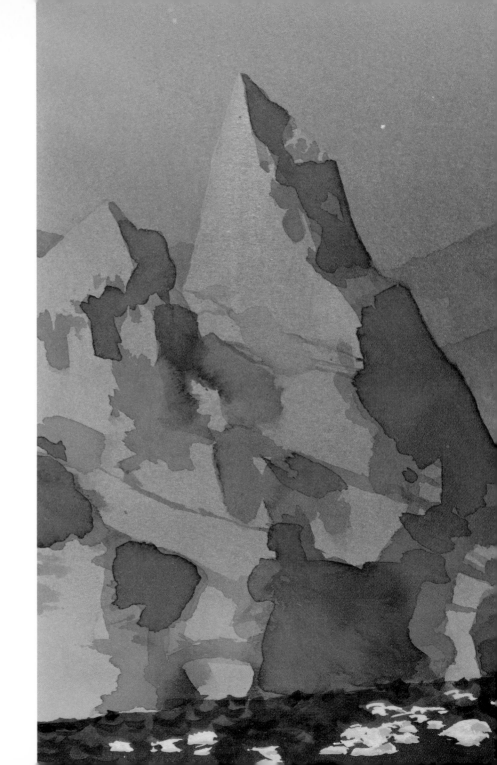

But during the night the winds shifted. At early dawn Zack was startled awake by a jolting thump, then frantic barks from Salty.

Zack scrambled out of his sleeping bag. Salty's barks were getting farther and farther away.

"Salty where are you?" he shouted.

Salty had jumped onto a gigantic iceberg and was drifting out to sea!

Zack quickly untied the dinghy and rowed as fast as he could after his crew. Oh, Salty, he thought, icebergs aren't for riding. They're slippery. If you fall off, there'll be no way to save you.

Using all his strength, Zack caught up with the moving iceberg. He pulled alongside and yelled at Salty: *"Jump! Jump!"*

Salty stood shaking on the iceberg. Zack saw the fear in his eyes, but he counted on Salty's obeying an order. *"Now, Salty! Jump!"*

Salty made a big leap and tumbled into the dinghy.

"It's okay, it's okay," Zack soothed in a soft voice, hugging his shivering dog. "You scared the wits out of me. I'm so glad to have you back. What would I ever do if anything happened to my crew?"

Salty licked Zack's face over and over, whimpering happy whimpers.

That evening, anchored in a sheltered bay, they watched the northern lights play magic colors across the sky.

"Tomorrow we sail into the next town's harbor and tie up for the winter," Zack told Salty. "The days are getting shorter and colder. We'll live ashore for a while. Winter is no time to be out at sea."

Salty cocked his head as if he understood.

"You've been a great crew on a long, rugged cruise." Zack saluted Salty as they stepped ashore the next day. "You learned a lot about the sea, a lot about the wilderness, and a lot about being brave. I'll sign you on again as my crew any day."

Salty barked a quick bark, as if to say "Aye, aye, sir," like any good salty dog would do.